*All children have
a great ambition to read
to themselves . . .*

*and a sense of achievement when they can do so.
The* **read it yourself** *series has been devised to
satisfy their ambition. Since many children learn
from the Ladybird Key Words Reading Scheme,
these stories have been based to a large extent
on the Key Words List, and the tales chosen are
those with which children are likely to be familiar.*

*The series can of course be used as
supplementary reading for any reading scheme.*
Peter and the Wolf *is intended for children reading
up to Book 3c of the Ladybird Reading Scheme.
The following words are additional to the
vocabulary used at that level –*

meadow, but, gate, closed, bird, sings,
opens, duck, she, swim, from, silly, can't,
fly, argue, cat, near, out, flies, away,
safe, grandfather, takes, wolf, not, may,
of, after, swallows, gulp, goes, round,
inside, rope, him, ties, lets, hunters, zoo

*A list of other titles at the same level will be
found on the back cover.*

Published by Ladybird Books Ltd Loughborough Leicestershire UK
Ladybird Books Inc Lewiston Maine 04240 USA

© LADYBIRD BOOKS LTD MCMLXXVIII

Peter and the Wolf

by Fran Hunia
illustrated by Kathie Layfield

Ladybird Books

Peter is at home.

He wants to go and play
in the meadow,
but the gate is closed.

A bird is up in the tree

in the meadow.

The bird sings to Peter,

Come on, Peter.

Come into the meadow.

Yes, says Peter.

Here I come.

He opens the gate

and goes into the meadow.

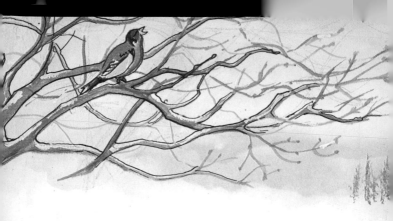

Peter plays in the meadow.

The bird sings
up in the tree.

A duck comes
into the meadow.

She goes for a swim
in the water.

The bird flies down
from the tree.

He says to the duck,
You are a silly bird.
You can't fly.
See, I can fly.

The duck says to the bird,

You are a silly bird.

You can't swim.

See, I can swim.

They argue and argue.

A cat comes up.

He sees the duck
and the bird.
I want that bird,
he says.

The duck and the bird
argue and argue.

They can't see the cat.

The cat gets near

to the duck and the bird.

Peter sees the cat.

Look out! he says.

The bird flies up
into the tree.

The duck swims away.

They are safe.

The cat looks up at the bird.

Out comes Peter's
grandfather.

Come here, Peter,
he says.
You have to come home
with me.
It is not safe out here
in the meadow.
A wolf may come
and get you.

Grandfather takes Peter
out of the meadow.

They go home
and Grandfather closes
the gate.

A wolf comes out
into the meadow.

He sees the cat, the duck
and the bird.

The cat sees the wolf

and jumps up

into the tree,

with the bird.

They are safe.

The duck sees the wolf.

She jumps out of the water and runs away.

The wolf runs after the duck

29

The wolf gets the duck
and swallows it down
in one gulp.

The cat and the bird
are up in the tree.

They are safe.

The wolf goes
round and round the tree
but he can't get up.

Peter looks out
into the meadow
and sees the wolf.

He goes inside
to get a rope.

Peter takes the rope

up into the tree.

He is going

to get the wolf.

Peter says to the bird,

Fly round the wolf,

please.

I want to get him

with this rope.

The bird flies down.

The bird flies

round and round the wolf.

Peter ties the rope

to the tree.

He lets the rope down.

Peter gets the wolf.

The wolf jumps up and dow

He can't get away.

Some hunters come.

They are looking

for the wolf.

Look, says Peter.

Here is the wolf.

He can't get away.

Please help me

to take him

to the zoo.

They all go to the zoo.

Peter and the bird . . .

the hunters with the wolf . .

Grandfather . . .

and the cat.